一九九五、九、十。共小平參觀
此界農場於展覽得此素食譜
現引吃素試做素食供老同人。

志賢誌之。

VERY! VERY! VEGETARIAN!

CHINESE STYLE

AUTHOR
Chen-Hsia Wang

EDITOR
Huang Su-Huei

EDITORIAL STAFF
Sophia Lin
Yen-Jen Lai
John Holt

TRANSLATION
Innie Hua

ART DIRECTION
F.S. Chang

PHOTOGRAPHY
Aki Ohno

DESIGN
AGP Productions Inc.

WEI-CHUAN PUBLISHING
1455 Monterey Pass Rd., #110
Monterey Park, CA 91754, U.S.A.
Tel: (213)261-3880 (213)261-3878
Fax: (213)261-3299

2nd Fl., 28 Section 4 Jen-Ai Road
Taipei, Taiwan, R.O.C.
Tel: (02)702-1148 (02)702-1149
Fax: (02)704-2729

PRINTED IN TAIWAN, R.O.C.

FIRST PRINTING, OCTOBER 1994
ISBN 0-941676-51-X

作者
王鎮俠

總編輯
黃淑惠

文稿協助
林淑華、賴燕眞、何久恩

翻譯
華茵

設計策劃
張方馨

攝影
大野現

設計
AGP Productions Inc.

電腦排版
甘露資訊印刷有限公司

印刷
中華彩色印刷股份有限公司

味全出版社有限公司
台北市仁愛路4段28號2樓
郵政劃撥00182038號味全出版社帳戶
電話： (02) 702-1148. (02) 702-1149
傳眞： (02) 704-2729

版權所有
局版台業字第0179號
中華民國83年10月初版
定價：新台幣壹佰貳拾元整

Contents 目 錄

Conversion Tables 量 器 介 紹

1 C. (1 cup) = 236 c.c.   *1杯 = 236 c.c.*

1 T. (1 tablespoon) = 15 c.c.   *1大匙 = 15 c.c.*

1 t. (1 teaspoon) = 5 c.c.   *1小匙 = 5 c.c.*

Recipe measurements in this book (pp. 8 thru 77) are designed for two servings.

本食譜份量爲二人份

- To prepare a meal for 2 persons, select two dishes and complete the meal with a soup or dessert. To achieve a balanced diet, select five different colored vegetarian ingredients for the daily menu.

- When trying a recipe for the first time, follow the instructions, timing, and quantities in this book. Recipes may be revised later according to personal taste, preference and ingredient availability.

- 擬定二人菜單時，可選二菜另加湯或點心；爲使營養均衡，每日菜單儘量選用五種不同顏色的素食材料。

- 初學者宜依照本書之份量及方法，熟練後即可依自己的喜好以手邊現有材料相互取代，自行變化。

□　　　　　　　□　　　　　　　□　　　　　　　□

1 | 10 Chinese black mushrooms
　　　(presoftened, shredded)
　　　$^1/_2$ c. chick peas

$^2/_3$ lb. (300g) stems of buttered
nappa cabbage

1 | 香菇（泡軟、切絲）…………10朶
　　鷄豆 ……………………………$^1/_2$杯

白菜（菜梗）………8兩（300公克）

🌊　🌊　🌊

1 | 1 c. Chinese black mushroom
　　　stems (see p. 17, procedure *1*)

$^1/_2$ lb. (225g) bean sprouts
$^2/_3$ lb. (300g) presoftened, shredded
seaweed
5 slices ginger root

香菇蒂（見17頁作法 *1*）………1杯

1 | 黃豆芽 ……………6兩（225公克）
　　海帶絲（泡好的）…8兩（300公克）
　　薑 ………………………………5片

🌊　🌊　🌊

1 | 1 ear of corn, cut in sections,retain
　　　stringy fiber
　　　1 Italian squash, sliced
　　　8 mushrooms, sliced

1 | 玉米（切段，保留皮、鬚）…1條
　　義大利瓜（切片）…………1條
　　洋菇（切片）…………………8粒

Flavorful Vegetarian Stock
鮮味素高湯

Makes 6 cups　6杯

1 Heat 2 T. oil; stir-fry **1** . Add nappa cabbage and stir-fry briefly. Add 8 c. water then bring to boil. Reduce heat to low and continue cooking 15 minutes. Strain the liquid.

1 油2大匙燒熱，炒香 **1** 料，隨入白菜略炒軟，加水8杯用大火燒開，改小火蓋鍋煮15分鐘，再將湯瀝出即成。

Vegetarian Seaweed Stock
海味素高湯

Makes 6 cups　6杯

1 Heat 2 T. oil; stir-fry mushroom stems until fragrant. Add **1** and stir-fry briefly. Add 8 c. water then bring to boil. Reduce heat to low, cover, and cook 15 minutes. Strain the liquid.

1 油2大匙燒熱，炒香香菇蒂，隨入 **1** 料略炒，加水8杯用大火燒開，改小火蓋鍋煮15分鐘，再將湯瀝出即成。

Clear Vegetarian Stock
清味素高湯

Makes 6 cups　6杯

1 Add 8 c. water to **1** then bring to boil. Reduce heat to low, cover, and cook 15 minutes. Strain the liquid.

■ Outer leaves and bottom stems of vegetables may be saved and used to make vegetarian stock. Vegetables retained after straining the stock may be used to make a secondary stock. Just add water and cook.

1 將 **1** 料加水8杯大火燒開，改小火蓋鍋煮15分鐘瀝出即爲無油之素高湯。

■ 煮素高湯時，可將外葉、菜根等廢物利用；湯內不加其他調味料，才能保持湯之甘香。第一次瀝出之渣澤，可再加水燒煮即爲次高湯。

5

1 vegetarian chicken (see p. 45)

oil for deep-frying

1
- 2 star anises
- $1/2$ t. Szechwan peppercorns
- $1/4$ fresh lemon skin
  or orange skin
- $1/4$ t. cinnamon powder

2
- 2 t. sugar
- 3 slices ginger
- 6 T. soy sauce
- 4 c. water

3
- 2 gluten rolls (see p. 61)
- 4 rolls presoftened seaweed, 6"
  (15cm) long, (roll up and
  secure with toothpick)
- 1 slice pressed bean curd
  (see p. 31)

coriander, sesame oil as desired

	素鷄（見45頁）	⋯⋯⋯⋯⋯1個
	炸油	⋯⋯⋯⋯⋯⋯⋯適量
1	八角	⋯⋯⋯⋯⋯⋯⋯2朵
	花椒粒	⋯⋯⋯⋯⋯⋯1/2小匙
	新鮮檸檬皮或橘皮	⋯⋯⋯⋯1/4個
	肉桂粉	⋯⋯⋯⋯⋯⋯1/4小匙
2	糖	⋯⋯⋯⋯⋯⋯⋯2小匙
	薑	⋯⋯⋯⋯⋯⋯⋯3片
	醬油	⋯⋯⋯⋯⋯⋯6大匙
	水	⋯⋯⋯⋯⋯⋯⋯4杯
3	麵筋（見61頁）	⋯⋯⋯⋯2條
	濕海帶（15公分長，捲起用牙籤固定）	⋯⋯⋯⋯⋯4卷
	豆乾（見31頁）	⋯⋯⋯⋯1片
	香菜、麻油	⋯⋯⋯⋯各少許

Vegetarian Platter

滷素拼盤

1 Heat oil for deep-frying. Fry vegetarian chicken in medium heat until golden brown.

2 Heat 4 T. oil; bring **1** and **2** to boil. Add the chicken and **3** ; boil again. Reduce heat to medium; continue to cook 15 minutes. Remove and slice; sprinkle with coriander and sesame oil.

■ Deep-frying chicken before cooking prevents separation during cooking. Liquid from cooking the chicken may be retained for other uses. Ready-made stewing pouch may be used for **1** .

1 炸油燒熱，用中火將素鷄炸至表面微黃備用。

2 油4大匙燒熱加 **1** 、 **2** 料燒開，隨入素鷄及 **3** 料再燒開，改中火續煮15分鐘取出，切片撒上香菜、麻油即成。

■ 將素鷄炸過後再滷，才不易散開。剩餘的滷汁可以再用；市面上有售現成的滷包，可用來取代 **1** 料。

¹/₂ c. mashed potatoes*

1 total of 2 lb. (900g), diced: cooked potatoes & carrot, American vegetarian ham (see p. 55), gherkin cucumber, honeydew, apple, and 2 boiled eggs

2 ¹/₂ lb. (225g) mayonnaise
1 T. each: sugar, lemon juice

¹/₂ lb. (225g) wet shredded seaweed

1 total of ¹/₂ lb. (225g), shredded: chayote, carrot, celery

2 ¹/₄ c. fresh ginger root, shredded
2 slices Japanese vegetarian ham, shredded (see p. 33)
1 T. each: vinegar, sesame oil and oil
1 t. sugar
¹/₂ t. salt

(see p. 55) (see p. 33)

馬鈴薯泥* ·················¹/₂杯

1
熟馬鈴薯、熟紅蘿蔔、
美國素火腿（見55頁）、
小黃瓜、哈蜜瓜、蘋果、
熟鷄蛋2個 …共1斤半（900公克）

2
美乃滋 ··············6兩（225公克）
糖、檸檬汁 ···········各1大匙

Vegetarian Salad

素味沙拉

1　Mix  ¹ , ² , and mashed potatoes; stir to mix well. Serve.

★　To make 1/2 c. of mashed potatoes: mix 1/2 c. potato powder with 1/2 c. boiling water.

1　將 ¹ 料切丁，加 ² 料及馬鈴薯泥混合拌勻即成素味沙拉。

★　馬鈴薯泥¹/₂杯，即買現成的馬鈴薯粉¹/₂杯，加滾水¹/₂杯攪拌。

濕海帶絲 ··············6兩（225公克）

1
佛手瓜、紅蘿蔔、西芹
···········切絲共6兩（225公克）

2
薑絲 ···························¹/₄杯
日本素火腿（見33頁，切絲） 2片
醋、麻油、沙拉油 ······各1大匙
糖······1小匙，鹽 ·········¹/₂小匙

Shredded Seaweed Salad

涼拌海帶絲

1　Cut seaweed to 3" (8cm) in length. Put in boiling water; bring to boil again. Remove immediately; drain.

2　Marinate ¹ with 1 t. salt 10 minutes. Add in ² and seaweed; stir to mix well. May add red chili as desired.

1　將濕海帶絲切8公分長，放入滾水內燒開即取出，瀝乾水份。

2　將 ¹ 料加鹽1小匙醃10分鐘，加入 ² 料及海帶絲一起拌勻即成。紅辣椒隨意。

9

4 sheets nori (see p. 73)

2 c. hot cooked rice

1 t. cooked black sesame seeds
1 T. each: sugar, lemon juice (or vinegar), vegetarian oil
¼ t. salt

4 slices vegetarian ham, cut in strips, fried briefly
4 branches spinach, rinsed and cooked
1 T. shredded red ginger root*
4 long sections pickled radish*

1 bamboo sushi mat

10

紫菜（見73頁）⋯⋯⋯⋯⋯⋯4張

熱蓬來米飯 ⋯⋯⋯⋯⋯⋯⋯2杯

1

炒熟的黑芝麻 ⋯⋯⋯⋯⋯1小匙
糖、檸檬汁或醋、素油 各1大匙
鹽 ⋯⋯⋯⋯⋯⋯⋯⋯⋯¹/₄小匙

2

素火腿(切條、略煎) ⋯⋯⋯4片
菠菜(洗淨、燙熟) ⋯⋯⋯⋯4棵
紅薑絲 ⋯⋯⋯⋯⋯⋯⋯⋯1大匙
黃蘿蔔 ⋯⋯⋯⋯⋯⋯⋯⋯4長條

竹簾 ⋯⋯⋯⋯⋯⋯⋯⋯⋯⋯1張

Nori Rolls

紫菜捲

1   Lightly stir and mix rice with **1** well; divide in 4 portions when cooled. (Reduce amount of water when cooking rice for this recipe.)

2   Place nori on sushi mat then spread rice on half the nori. Put **2** in center of rice; roll up to form a baton. Then seal with rice. Tightly stuff both ends with rice.

3   Cut nori rolls into sections with wet knife and serve with mixed soy sauce and mustard sauce.

⋆   Red ginger root and pickled yellow radish are available in oriental markets.

1   將飯與 **1** 料輕拌均勻，待冷後分成4份。(煮飯時水量要比一般量減少)。

2   竹簾上置紫菜，取一份拌好的飯，均勻的平鋪在紫菜的半邊位置，將 **2** 料排在飯中央，捲成圓筒狀黏合，兩端用米粒塞緊。

3   刀口沾水，將紫菜捲切成段，可沾醬油拌芥末醬食用。

1. 30 cooked chick peas
   10 cooked Chinese red dates
   total of ⅓ lb. (150g): yam, carrot, seaweed or nori, wheat, pine nuts (Fig. 1)

2. total of ⅔ lb. (300g): sesame seeds, alfalfa sprouts, malabar spinach (Fig. 2), diced tomatoes, shredded purple cabbage & lettuce, sliced apples

3. 2 T. lemon juice
   1 T. each: honey, olive oil

1

1	鷄豆（煮熟） ························30粒 紅棗（煮熟） ························10粒 番薯、紅蘿蔔、海帶或紫菜、 麥粒、松子（圖1）共4兩（150公克）	
2	苜蓿芽、皇宮菜（圖2）、番茄（切 丁）、紫色高麗菜絲、生菜絲、蘋 果（切片）········共8兩（300公克）	
3	檸檬汁 ···························2大匙 蜂蜜 ·····························1大匙 橄欖油 ···························1大匙	

Healthy Eating I

健康生食 I

1 To prepare **1** : Cook yam and carrot; dice. Soften seaweed in water then cut in pieces; blanch. Soak the wheat in warm water for 1 day; drain. Cover with wet cloth for 1 day until sprouted. Stir-fry the pine nuts until cooked.

2 Place **1** and **2** on a plate; mix with mixture **3** when ready to eat. Salt is not needed in this dish.

1 將番薯、紅蘿蔔分別煮熟、切丁。海帶泡軟切塊燙熟。麥粒用溫水泡一天瀝出後以濕布蓋好放置一天，使其出芽。松子炒熟備用。

2 將 **1** 料及 **2** 料裝在盤上，此道菜不用鹽，食時拌入調勻的 **3** 料即可。

Healthy Eating II

健康生食 II

1 Separately cook lotus seeds, diced taro and chayote, green bean sprouts, on choy, Taiwan bok choy; mix in germinated rice, raisins, cashews, diced avocado, and beet. Total 1 lb. (450g) of all these mixed ingredients. Add in 1 T. each of ketchup, olive oil, and lemon juice; stir to mix well.

1 蓮子、芋頭丁、佛手瓜丁、綠豆芽、空心菜、小白菜，分別煮熟加糙米飯、奶菓丁、紅甜菜丁、葡萄乾、腰果共1磅（450公克）拌入番茄醬、橄欖油、檸檬汁各1大匙即可。

2

13

¼ lb. (115g) Chinese black mushrooms

1 ½ T. beet juice (beet, see Fig. 2)

1 | ¼ t. salt
   | 1 egg, beaten
   | 1 T. each: soy sauce, cornstarch
   | ½ t. pepper, sesame oil
   | ¼ t. five spice powder (optional)

2 | total of ¼ lb. (115g): green bean
   | sprouts (remove roots), shred-
   | ded bamboo shoots, or other
   | vegetables

oil for deep-frying

14

香菇 ·················3兩(115公克)

紅甜菜汁(圖2,擠出汁) 1 ¹/₂大匙

1
鹽 ·······························¹/₄小匙
蛋(打散) ·······················1個
醬油、太白粉 ··········各1大匙
胡椒、麻油 ··············各¹/₂小匙
五香粉(無亦可) ···········¹/₄小匙

2
綠豆芽(摘除根部)、筍絲、
或其他蔬菜······共3兩(115公克)

炸油 ·························適量

Vegetarian Eel

乾炒素鱔

1 Soften the mushrooms in cold water; squeeze out water to yield a net weight of 3/4 lb. (340g). Cut each mushroom along the edge to form long strips then cut in 2" (5cm) sections (Fig. 1). Add in beet juice for color then add mixture **1**; stir to mix well.

2 Heat oil for deep-frying; fry the mushrooms over high heat 2 minutes. Remove.

3 Heat 1 T. oil. Stir-fry **2** briefly. Add fried mushrooms; stir to mix well.

1 將香菇泡軟,擠乾水份(約9兩,340公克);沿香菇邊緣剪成長條狀(圖1)後切5公分長段,先拌入甜菜汁(上顏色用),再加調勻的 **1** 料拌勻。

2 炸油燒熱,用大火將香菇炸2分鐘(不必炸很乾),撈出備用。

3 油1大匙燒熱,將 **2** 料略炒,再加炸好的香菇炒拌均勻即成。

2

1 c. Chinese black mushroom stems

1. ¼ t. each: salt, pepper
1 T. soy sauce
1 T. cornstarch
1 egg

2. ½ lb. (225g) pickled mustard cabbage, cut in strips
¼ c. carrot, cut in strips

16

乾香菇蒂 ……………………1杯

1
鹽、胡椒 ………………各¼小匙
醬油、太白粉 …………各1大匙
蛋 ……………………………1個

2
酸菜(切條) ………6兩(225公克)
紅蘿蔔(切條) …………………¼杯

Pickled Cabbage & Beef

酸菜素牛肉

1. Soak mushroom stems in hot water over night until soft. Cut off hard bottom portion. Rinse and squeeze out water then flatten (Fig. 1); yield is about 1/4 lb. (115g). Mix with **1**.

2. Heat 4 T. oil. Fry mushroom stems over high heat until slightly brown. Remove stems.

3. Use remaining oil to stir-fry **2** in medium heat. Remove and put on a plate; place the stems on top. Serve.

1. 香菇蒂是菇傘下的長柱部份，使用時用熱水隔夜泡軟後切除底部硬塊洗淨，擠乾水份搥扁(圖1)約3兩(115公克)，拌入 **1** 料。

2. 油4大匙燒熱，將香菇蒂大火煎炒呈微黃。

3. 餘油將 **2** 料炒熱，上置炒好的香菇蒂即成。

Vegetarian Seafood

素炒三鮮

1. Mix total 1/4 lb. (115g) of sliced gluten rolls and Chinese black mushroom stems with **1** then follow procedures **1** & **2** above.

2. Use Chinese pea pods, mushrooms, and red pepper for ingredients **2**. Stir-fry briefly. Place the mushroom stems on top and serve.

1. 將麵筋片及香菇蒂共3兩(115公克)拌入 **1** 料，依上面做法 **1**、**2** 炒呈微黃。

2. **2** 料改用豌豆莢、洋菇、紅椒略炒，置香菇蒂上即成。

17

2 c. medium size Chinese black mushrooms

¼ lb. (115g) canned golden mushrooms

¼ lb. (115g) snow pea leaves or spinach

1 | ½ t. salt
    2 t. cornstarch

2 | 1 T. sugar
    2 T. soy sauce

中型香菇	....	2杯
金針菇(罐頭)	......	3兩(115公克)
豆苗或波菜	....	3兩(115公克)

1
鹽	....	1/2小匙
太白粉	....	2小匙

2
糖	....	1大匙
醬油	....	2大匙

Authentic Chinese Mushrooms

一品香菇

1 Cut black mushrooms in half (do not soak in water); squeeze water from golden mushrooms (Fig. 1).

2 Heat 2 T. oil. Add golden mushrooms and snow pea leaves; stir-fry briefly. Sprinkle **1** ; stir to mix well. Remove.

3 Heat 8 T. oil. Add black mushrooms; turn off heat and stir-fry 3 minutes. Add mixture **2** and stir to mix well; remove and place on top of cooked vegetables. Serve. Chinese black mushrooms prepared this way retain their original flavor.

1 將香菇切半(不可泡水)。金針菇(圖1)擠乾水份備用。

2 油2大匙燒熱,依序入金針菇、豆苗略炒,再撒入 **1** 料炒拌均勻後盛出。

3 油8大匙燒熱,入香菇立即熄火,將香菇炒3分鐘後,加入調勻的 **2** 料拌勻,置於炒好的蔬菜上即成。此種香菇做法可保有原始香味,愈嚼愈香。

½ lb. (225g) presoftened sea-
    weed knots*

1 c. fried bean curd (Fig. 1),
    sliced

½ c. sugar snow peas or celery

6 ginger root slices

¼ t. each: salt, pepper
1 T. each: B.B.Q. (Sa Tsa) sauce
    (see p. 31), soy sauce
2 T. stock or water

1

Fried Seaweed Knots

炒海帶結

泡好的海帶結* …6兩（225公克）

油豆腐（圖1，切片）…………1杯

甜豆或芹菜 ……………………¹/₂杯

薑 ………………………………6片

鹽、胡椒 ………………各¹/₄小匙
沙茶醬（見31頁）、醬油 各1大匙
高湯或水 ………………………2大匙

1. Separately put seaweed knots and fried bean curd in boiling water; boil again. Remove and drain.

2. Heat 1/2 T. oil. Add snow peas (add 1 T. water if too dry) and stir-fry briefly. Remove and wipe the wok dry.

3. Heat 3 T. oil. Stir-fry ginger. Add seaweed knots and fried bean curd; stir. Add mixture **1** and snow peas; stir to mix well.

* Soak dried seaweed knots (Fig. 2) in water for 2 hours, clean, then rinse to remove stickiness; they should expand to 5 or 6 times original size.

1. 海帶結與油豆腐（圖1）分別放入滾水內川燙即撈出。

2. 油¹/₂大匙燒熱，入甜豆，如太乾加水1大匙略炒後盛出，擦乾鍋面。

3. 油3大匙燒熱，炒香薑片，依序入海帶結、油豆腐炒熱，再加調勻的 **1** 料及炒好的甜豆炒拌均勻即成。

* 乾海帶結（圖2），使用時需泡水約2小時，並洗去黏液，泡過後約增5或6倍。

2

1.
½ lb. (225g) vegetarian cuttle-fish*
1 c. celery (cut to 1" (2cm) long)

2.
1 T. dried chili, diagonally cut in slices
1 T. pickled mustard greens, minced

3.
¼ t. salt
2 t. each: sugar, cornstarch
1 t. vinegar
1 ½ T. soy sauce
3 T. water

½ c. roasted peanuts

1

22

素魷魚* ··········6兩(225公克)
1
西芹(切2公分長) ············1杯

乾辣椒(切斜片) ··········1大匙
2
榨菜(切碎) ·············1大匙

鹽 ····················¼小匙
糖、太白粉 ·········各2小匙
3
醋 ····················1小匙
醬油 ·················1½大匙
水 ····················3大匙

熟花生米 ···············½杯

Spicy Cuttlefish

宮保素魷

1   Heat 3 T. oil. Stir-fry **2** until fragrant; add **1** and stir. Add mixture **3** then stir to mix well. Add peanuts and stir lightly.

*   Vegetarian cuttlefish is made of konnyaku powder and sodium carbonate. To create a design, cut crisscross on surface of cuttlefish (Fig. 1). Secure with tooth-pick (Fig. 2) then cook 5 minutes in boiling water to set the shape. Ready-made vegetarian cuttlefish is available in oriental markets.

1   油3大匙燒熱，炒香 **2** 料，隨入 **1** 料炒熱，續入調勻的 **3** 料炒拌均勻，再加花生略炒拌即成。

*   素魷魚是蒟蒻粉加食用碱水製成，切花時可在表面直或斜交叉劃刀，再用竹籤固定(圖1、2)，放入滾水煮5分鐘定形；市面上有現成的出售。

2

²/₃ lb. (300g) vegetarian cuttlefish balls or vegetarian meat balls

½ c. gluten rolls, diagonally cut in slices

1 total of ⅓ lb. (150g): green bell pepper or celery, bamboo shoot, carrot, sliced
hot chili as desired
⅛ t. salt

2 2 T. sweet bean paste
1 T. each: soy sauce, sesame oil
1 t. vinegar

1

Cuttlefish Balls

醬爆素腰花

素花枝丸或素貢丸 8兩(300公克)

麵筋(切斜片) ⋯⋯⋯⋯⋯⋯1/2杯

1

青椒或芹菜、筍、紅蘿蔔
⋯⋯⋯⋯切片共4兩(150公克)
紅辣椒 ⋯⋯⋯⋯⋯⋯⋯⋯⋯隨意
鹽 ⋯⋯⋯⋯⋯⋯⋯⋯⋯⋯1/8小匙

2

甜麵醬 ⋯⋯⋯⋯⋯⋯⋯⋯2大匙
醬油、麻油 ⋯⋯⋯⋯⋯各1大匙
醋 ⋯⋯⋯⋯⋯⋯⋯⋯⋯⋯⋯1小匙

1 Vegetarian cuttlefish balls (Fig. 1) are made of konnyaku powder and sodium carbonate. Cut the balls in flower shapes.

2 Heat 1 T. oil. Add gluten rolls then **1** (add 1 T. water if too dry); stir-fry briefly. Remove; place on a plate.

3 Heat 3 T. oil. Stir-fry the cuttlefish until hot. Add mixture **2** and stir to mix well. Place on top of cooked vegetables. Serve.

1 素花枝丸(圖1,是以蒟蒻粉加食用碱水製成)切花。

2 油1大匙燒熱,先入麵筋再入 **1** 料,如太乾加水1大匙略炒後盛出裝盤。

3 油3大匙燒熱,將素花枝丸炒熱,再加調勻的 **2** 料炒拌均勻,置在炒好的蔬菜上即成。

2 slices toast, diced

¼ c. Japanese vegetarian ham (see p. 33, diced)
2 beaten eggs
1 t. sesame oil
1 t. minced basil powder or fresh basil (see p. 69)

total of ½ lb. (225g), diced carrots & gherkin cucumber, chick peas (see p. 57)

1 T. soy sauce

土司麵包（切丁）⋯⋯⋯⋯2片

1
日本素火腿（見33頁，切丁）¹/₄杯
蛋（打散）⋯⋯⋯⋯⋯⋯⋯⋯2個
麻油 ⋯⋯⋯⋯⋯⋯⋯⋯⋯1小匙
新鮮九層塔（見69頁）切碎
或九層粉 ⋯⋯⋯⋯⋯⋯1小匙

2
紅蘿蔔、小黃瓜（切丁）、
鷄豆（見57頁） 共6兩（225公克）

醬油 ⋯⋯⋯⋯⋯⋯⋯⋯1大匙

Stir-fried Toast

香炒土司

1 Mix the toast with **1** .

2 Heat 3 T. oil. Stir-fry toast until brown; remove.

3 Heat 1 t. oil. Stir-fry **2** briefly. Add the toast and soy sauce; stir to mix well.

1 將麵包丁拌入 **1** 料備用。

2 油3大匙燒熱，將拌好的麵包丁半煎炒至微黃盛出。

3 油1小匙燒熱，入 **2** 料略炒，再加炒好的麵包及醬油炒拌均勻即成。

²/₃ lb. (300g) Chinese broccoli, sectioned

total of ¹/₃ lb. (150g): Chinese black mushrooms (presoftened and cut in half) and canned straw mushrooms

1 | ¹/₂ t. salt
3 T. water

🍂　🍂　🍂

1 | ¹/₄ lb. (115g) fresh soybeans (see p. 51)
¹/₄ lb. (115g) bean curd pouch*, cut in strips

¹/₂ lb. (225g) gai choy

2 | 1 t. cornstarch
¹/₃ c. water

1

芥蘭菜(切段) ……8兩(300公克)

香菇(泡軟，切半)、
草菇(罐頭) ……共4兩(150公克)

1 鹽 …………………………¹/₂小匙
水 …………………………3大匙

毛豆(見51頁) ……3兩(115公克)
1 新鮮腐皮*(切條)　3兩(115公克)

芥菜 ………………6兩(225公克)

太白粉 ……………………1小匙
2 水 …………………………¹/₃杯

Chinese Broccoli & Mushrooms

雙菇芥蘭

1 Heat 3 T. oil then stir-fry black mushrooms until fragrant. Add broccoli and straw mushrooms; stir-fry briefly. Add **1** and stir to mix well.

1 油3大匙燒熱，炒香香菇，隨入芥蘭菜及草菇略炒，再加 **1** 料炒拌均勻即成。

Cabbage & Bean Curd Pouch

雪菜腐衣

1 Cut gai choy to 0.5" (1.5cm) wide. Add 2 t. salt then rub gai choy 10 minutes until soft, let stand for 10 minutes. Squeeze out water to make pickled cabbage.

2 Heat 3 T. oil. Stir-fry **1** ; add pickled cabbage and stir-fry briefly. Add mixture **2** ; stir-fry and mix well.

★ Bean curd pouch (Fig. 1) is made by mashing soybeans with water, removing membrane formed on top, then folding the membrane to make a square (also called fu pea).

1 芥菜切1.5公分寬，加鹽2小匙搓揉至菜軟放10分鐘，擠乾水份即成雪菜。

2 油3大匙燒熱，入 **1** 料炒熱，隨入雪菜略炒，再加調勻的 **2** 料拌炒均勻即成。

★ 新鮮腐皮(圖1)是黃豆加水磨成漿後浮在表面凝成一層薄膜，再挑起並折疊起來的方塊，又稱豆包。

1. total of ²/₃ lb. (300g): Chinese celery (cut in sections), carrot (cut in strips)
   ⅛ t. salt

2. total of ⅓ lb. (150g, cut in strips): vegetarian meat (see p. 53) (optional), pressed bean curd (Fig. 1)

3. 1 T. each: soy sauce, vegetarian sa tsa sauce*
   1 t. sesame oil

1

中國芹菜(切段)
紅蘿蔔(切條) … 共8兩(300公克)
鹽 …………………………¹/₈小匙

素五花肉(見53頁)、豆乾(圖1)
……………切條共4兩(150公克)

醬油、素沙茶醬* ………各1大匙
麻油 …………………………1小匙

Meat & Celery

五花香芹

1 Heat 1 1/2 T. oil. Add **1** (add 1 T. water if too dry); stir-fry briefly. Remove; wipe wok dry.

2 Heat 1 T. oil. Stir-fry **2** until yellowish; add mixture **3** then stir-fry briefly. Add cooked **1** and stir to mix well.

★ Vegetarian sa tsa (B.B.Q.) sauce (Fig. 2) is made of: Chinese black mushrooms, wheat powder, sesame powder, chili powder, and seasonings. This sauce enhances the flavor of a light dish and increases the appetite.

1 油1 ¹/₂大匙燒熱，入 **1** 料如太乾加水1大匙略炒盛出，擦乾鍋面。

2 油1大匙燒熱，將 **2** 料炒呈微黃(若無素五花肉可全部用豆乾)，隨入調勻的 **3** 料略炒，再加炒好的 **1** 料炒拌均勻即成。

★ 素沙茶醬(圖2)主要成份為香菇、麥粉、芝麻粉、辣椒粉及調味料，可使淡味的菜有香味並能增進食慾。

½ c. shredded Japanese
vegetarian ham*

1 | ⅔ lb. (300g) shredded potatoes
½ c. shredded Chinese pods

2 | ⅓ t. salt
1 T. sugar
1 T. vinegar

日本素火腿＊(切絲) ‥‥‥‥1/2杯

1 洋芋(馬鈴薯)切絲8兩(300公克)
豌豆莢(切絲) ‥‥‥‥‥‥1/2杯

2 鹽 ‥‥‥‥‥‥‥‥‥‥‥1/3小匙
糖 ‥‥‥‥‥‥‥‥‥‥‥1大匙
醋 ‥‥‥‥‥‥‥‥‥‥‥1大匙

Sweet & Sour Potato Shreds

醋溜芋絲

1 Soak potato shreds in water; drain before using.

2 Heat 2 T. oil. Stir-fry ham until yellowish; add **1** (add 1 T. water if too dry) and stir briefly. Add **2** and stir to mix well (potato shreds should be crispy).

★ Japanese vegetarian ham (Fig. 1) is made of soybeans. It may be shredded or diced.

1 將洋芋絲泡水(防止變黑)，使用前瀝乾水份。

2 油2大匙燒熱，將素火腿炒至微黃，隨入 **1** 料如太乾加水1大匙略炒，再加 **2** 料炒拌均勻即可(炒好的洋芋絲是脆的)。

★ 日本素火腿(圖1)是以大豆爲原料製成的，可切絲、切丁。

1. 1 1/3 lb. (600g) bitter melon
   straw mushrooms as desired,
   sliced

2. 1 T. fermented black beans*
   1 red chili, diagonally sliced

3. 1/4 t. salt
   1 T. each: sugar, water
   1 T. lemon juice or vinegar

1	苦瓜 ⋯⋯⋯⋯⋯⋯1斤(600公克)
	毛菇(切片) ⋯⋯⋯⋯⋯⋯⋯⋯隨意
2	豆豉 * ⋯⋯⋯⋯⋯⋯⋯⋯⋯⋯1大匙
	紅辣椒(切斜片) ⋯⋯⋯⋯⋯1條
3	鹽 ⋯⋯⋯⋯⋯⋯⋯⋯⋯⋯¼小匙
	糖、水 ⋯⋯⋯⋯⋯⋯⋯各1大匙
	檸檬汁或醋 ⋯⋯⋯⋯⋯1大匙

Flavored Bitter Melon

五味苦瓜

1 Remove melon seeds then cut in pieces, net weight is about 1 lb. (450g).

2 Heat 3 T. oil. Stir-fry **2** until fragrant; add **1** and stir-fry briefly. Add mixture **3** ; cover and cook until steamy. Stir melon until slightly cooked. To retain color and crispiness, do not overcook.

★ Fermented black beans (Fig. 1) are made by steaming and then fermenting black beans which have been marinated in salt water.

1 苦瓜去籽、切塊後約12兩(450公克)。

2 油3大匙燒熱,炒香 **2** 料,隨入 **1** 料略炒後,再加調勻的 **3** 料蓋鍋見水蒸氣冒出,炒拌至苦瓜略熟但仍清綠而脆即成。

★ 豆豉(圖1),是由黑豆蒸熟再經發酵加鹽水製成,鹹香開胃。

1 total of ½ lb. (225g), diced: pressed bean curd, American vegetarian ham (see p. 55), presoftened Chinese black mushrooms

2 total of ½ lb. (225g): green peas, diced chayote (or yam), potato, & red bell pepper

3 ¼ t. salt
1 t. soy sauce
¼ c. water

6 Chinese black mushrooms

2 T. soy sauce

½ lb. (225g) nappa cabbage or cabbage

1 2 oz. (50g) dried bean threads
½ c. water

Diced Vegetarian Mix
什錦素丁

1. 豆乾、美國素火腿(見55頁)
泡軟的香菇切丁共6兩(225公克)

2. 佛手瓜或涼薯、馬鈴薯、
紅椒(切丁)、青豆仁 ……共6兩
(225公克)

3. 鹽 ……………………………1/4小匙
醬油 …………………………1小匙
水 ……………………………1/4杯

1. Soak potato in water to prevent turning black; drain before use.

2. Heat 3 T. oil. Stir-fry **1** until fragrant; add **2** and stir until potato is heated. Add mixture **3** and stir-fry until mixed well and liquid is almost evaporated.

1. 將馬鈴薯泡水(防止變黑),使用前瀝乾水份。

2. 油3大匙燒熱,炒香 **1** 料,隨入 **2** 料炒至馬鈴薯略熱,再加調勻的 **3** 料炒拌均勻至汁略收乾即成。

Nappa Cabbage & Mushrooms
香菇白菜

香菇 ……………………………6朵

醬油 ……………………………2大匙

大白菜或高麗菜 …6兩(225公克)

1. 乾粉絲1小把 ……1.5兩(50公克)
水 ……………………………1/2杯

1. Soften mushrooms in cold water then shred;
slice cabbage. Soften bean threads in cold water; cut in half.

2. Heat 3 T. oil. Stir-fry mushrooms until fragrant; add soy sauce and nappa cabbage; stir-fry briefly. Add **1** ; bring to boil. Serve.

1. 香菇泡軟,切絲。大白菜切條。乾粉絲泡軟,略切備用。

2. 油3大匙燒熱,炒香香菇,依序入醬油、白菜略炒,再加 **1** 料燒開即成。

1 c. vegetarian meat chunks (see p. 71)

1
4 T. flour
1 T. each: cornstarch, sugar
¼ t. baking powder or baking soda
½ t. each: salt, pepper
1 egg
3 T. water

oil for deep-frying

1 T. sesame oil

2
3 T. ketchup
¼ t. each: salt, sugar
1 T. water

3
total of ½ lb. (225g), sliced: carrot, green bell pepper, pineapple

素肉塊（見71頁）⋯⋯⋯⋯⋯1杯

1
麵粉 ⋯⋯⋯⋯⋯⋯⋯⋯⋯4大匙
太白粉、糖 ⋯⋯⋯⋯⋯各1大匙
發粉或蘇打粉 ⋯⋯⋯⋯¹/₄小匙
鹽、胡椒 ⋯⋯⋯⋯⋯各¹/₂小匙
蛋 ⋯⋯⋯⋯⋯⋯⋯⋯⋯⋯1個
水 ⋯⋯⋯⋯⋯⋯⋯⋯⋯⋯3大匙

炸油 ⋯⋯⋯⋯⋯⋯⋯⋯⋯適量

麻油 ⋯⋯⋯⋯⋯⋯⋯⋯⋯1大匙

2
番茄醬 ⋯⋯⋯⋯⋯⋯⋯3大匙
鹽、糖 ⋯⋯⋯⋯⋯⋯各¹/₄小匙
水 ⋯⋯⋯⋯⋯⋯⋯⋯⋯⋯1大匙

3
紅蘿蔔、青椒、鳳梨
⋯⋯⋯⋯⋯切片共6兩（225公克）

Sweet & Sour Meat

咕咾素肉

1 Soften the meat in water yielding 1/2 lb. (225g). Mix well with mixture **1** .

2 Heat oil for deep-frying. Fry the marinated meat over high heat until brown; remove.

3 Heat 1 T. sesame oil. Add mixtures **2** and **3** ; bring to boil. Add the vegetarian meat; stir to mix well.

1 素肉塊1杯泡軟後約6兩（225公克），與調勻 **1** 料混合拌勻。

2 炸油燒熱，用大火將醃好的素肉塊炸至微黃撈出。

3 麻油1大匙燒熱，入調勻的 **2** 料及 **3** 料燒開，再加炸好的素肉塊拌炒均勻即成。

½ lb. (225g) Japanese or Chinese vegetarian ham (see p. 33)

1
½ c. flour
⅛ t. baking soda
1 egg
6 T. water

1 t. cedar leaves (see p. 69), minced

2
1 T. cornstarch
½ T. sesame oil
1 T. each: sweet bean paste, soy sauce
½ c. water

Shredded lettuce or white radish, as desired

Ham in Sauce

醬素排骨

日本或中國素火腿4片
（見33頁）⋯⋯⋯⋯6兩（225公克）

1
麵粉 ⋯⋯⋯⋯⋯⋯⋯⋯⋯⋯⋯⋯1/2杯
小蘇打粉 ⋯⋯⋯⋯⋯⋯⋯1/8小匙
蛋 ⋯⋯⋯⋯⋯⋯⋯⋯⋯⋯⋯⋯1個
水 ⋯⋯⋯⋯⋯⋯⋯⋯⋯⋯⋯⋯6大匙

香椿（見69頁，切碎）⋯⋯1小匙

2
太白粉 ⋯⋯⋯⋯⋯⋯⋯⋯⋯⋯1大匙
麻油 ⋯⋯⋯⋯⋯⋯⋯⋯⋯⋯1/2大匙
甜麵醬、醬油 ⋯⋯⋯⋯各1大匙
水 ⋯⋯⋯⋯⋯⋯⋯⋯⋯⋯⋯1/2杯

生菜或白蘿蔔 ⋯⋯⋯⋯⋯⋯適量

1 Mix **1** well to form a paste; add in vegetarian ham. Lay lettuce on a plate.

2 Heat 6 T. oil. Fry ham in medium heat until surface turns golden brown. Remove.

3 Heat 1 T. oil. Stir-fry cedar leaves; add mixture **2** then bring to boil. Add the ham; stir to mix well. Remove; place on top of lettuce.

1 將 **1** 料拌勻成糊狀，拌入素火腿。將生菜切絲鋪於盤底。

2 油6大匙燒熱，用中火將素火腿煎炸至表面呈金黃色撈出，即成素排骨。

3 油1大匙燒熱，炒香香椿末，隨入調勻的 **2** 料燒開，再入炸好的素排骨翻拌均勻盛出，置於生菜絲上即成。

½ lb. (225g) gluten puffs*

oil for deep-frying

1 | ¼ lb. (115g), sliced: bamboo shoots, presoftened Chinese black mushrooms & wood ears

2 | ½ t. pepper
1 T. each: sugar, soy sauce
2 T. vegetarian oyster sauce**
1 ½ c. vegetarian stock or water

3 T. green peas

烤麩 * ··············6兩（225公克）

炸油 ··············適量

泡好的香菇、木耳，及冬筍
··············切片共3兩（115公克）

胡椒 ··············1/2小匙
糖、醬油 ··············各1大匙
素蠔油 ** ··············2大匙
素高湯或水 ··············1 1/2杯

青豆仁 ··············3大匙

Gluten Puffs & Bamboo Shoots

雙冬烤麩

1 Cut gluten puffs in pieces.

2 Heat oil for deep-frying. Fry puffs in medium heat 4 minutes until golden brown and crispy. Remove puffs.

3 Use remaining 1 T. oil to stir-fry **1** briefly; add **2** and puffs. Bring to boil and cook until liquid is evaporated; add green peas and stir to mix well.

★ Gluten Puffs (Fig. 1) are made from gluten rolls.

★ ★Vegetarian oyster sauce (Fig. 2) is mainly made of Chinese black mushroom juice. It is rich in flavor and may be used as a dipping sauce.

1 將烤麩切塊備用。

2 炸油燒熱，用中火將烤麩炸呈金黃色酥脆約4分鐘撈出。

3 留油1大匙，將 **1** 料略炒，隨入 **2** 料及炸好的烤麩燒開，續煮至湯汁收乾，再加青豆仁略炒拌即成。

★ 烤麩（圖1）是麵筋發酵製成的。

★ ★素蠔油（圖2）主要成份是香菇汁，味鮮美，可當沾食的佐料。

⅔ lb. (300g) vegetarian chicken*,
cut to 0.5" (1cm) thick

1
½ t. salt
½ c. flour
1 egg
6 T. water

1 T. minced ginger root

½ c. sliced bamboo shoots
(optional)

2
1 T. cornstarch
1 t. sugar
1 T. vegetarian oyster sauce or
soy sauce paste
1 T. soy sauce
1 c. stock or water

3
2 nori sheets, minced
2 t. sesame oil

coriander as desired

素鷄*(切1公分厚)…8兩(300公克)

鹽	……………………………1/2小匙
麵粉	……………………………1/2杯
蛋	……………………………1個
水	……………………………6大匙

薑(切碎) …………………1大匙

筍片(無亦可) …………………1/2杯

太白粉	…………………1大匙
糖	…………………1小匙
素蠔油或醬油膏	…………1大匙
醬油	…………………1大匙
高湯或水	…………………1杯

紫菜(撕碎)	…………………2張
麻油	…………………2小匙

香菜 …………………隨意

Chicken & Nori

海味素鷄

1   Mix **1** together and stir to mix well to make paste.

2   Heat 4 T. oil. Coat vegetarian chicken with paste; fry over medium heat until both sides are yellowish. Remove and place on a plate.

3   Heat 1 T. oil. Stir-fry ginger until fragrant. Add bamboo shoots and stir briefly. Add mixture **2**; bring to boil and stir until sauce thickens. Add in chicken and **3**. Sprinkle on coriander.

★   Vegetarian chicken (Fig. 1) is made from bean curd skin which forms on top of cooled soy milk.

1   將 **1** 料拌勻成軟硬適中的麵糊。

2   油4大匙燒熱,素鷄沾裹麵糊,用中火煎至兩面微黃鏟出置盤。

3   油1大匙燒熱,炒香薑末,隨入筍片略炒,續入調勻的 **2** 料燒開,炒拌煮至濃稠狀,拌入煎好的素鷄及 **3** 料,上撒香菜即成。

★   素鷄(圖1)是豆漿上層因遇冷凝結的豆皮製成的。

1 lb. (450g) diced tofu

1 | 1 T. sesame oil
1 t. Szechwan peppercorns

2 | 1 t. minced ginger root
1 T. fermented black beans (see p. 35)
1 T. hot bean paste

3 | 1/4 t. salt
2 t. cornstarch
1 t. soy sauce
1/2 c. stock or water

豆腐(切丁)	……12兩(450公克)	

1	麻油	………………………1大匙
	花椒粒	………………………1小匙

2	薑(切碎)	………………………1小匙
	豆豉(見35頁)	……………1大匙
	辣豆瓣醬	…………………1大匙

3	鹽	…………………………¼小匙
	太白粉	……………………2小匙
	醬油	…………………………1小匙
	高湯或水	……………………½杯

Spicy Mao-Po Tofu

麻婆豆腐

1 Heat 2 T. oil. Stir-fry **1** over medium heat until fragrant. Remove peppercorns. Add in **2** and stir-fry until fragrant. Add tofu and mixture **3** . Bring to boil, stir 3 minutes until sauce thickens.

1 油2大匙燒熱，用中火將 **1** 料炒香後，花椒粒丟棄；餘油續炒香 **2** 料，隨入豆腐及調勻的 **3** 料燒開，炒拌煮至濃稠狀(約3分鐘)即成。

30 sheets dumpling skin

1 c. Chinese black mushroom
   stems

1 | ¹/₄ t. each: salt, pepper
   1 t. sesame oil
   1 egg

¹/₄ lb. (115g) Japanese vegetarian
   ham (see p. 33), diced

2 | total of 2 c., minced: cabbage,
   gai choy
   1 t. salt

3 | 2 t. flour
   ³/₄ c. water

4 | 1 T. soy sauce
   1 t. vinegar
   ¹/₄ t. sesame oil

水餃皮 ……………………30張

乾香菇蒂 …………………1杯

1 | 鹽、胡椒 ………………各¼小匙
麻油 ……………………1小匙
蛋 ………………………1個

日本素火腿(見33頁，切小丁)
…………………………3兩(115公克)

2 | 高麗菜、芥菜 ………切碎共2杯
鹽 ………………………1小匙

3 | 麵粉 ……………………2小匙
水 ………………………³/₄杯

4 | 醬油 ……………………1大匙
醋 ………………………1小匙
麻油 ……………………¼小匙

Fried Dumplings

素鍋貼

1 Soften mushroom stems in water then flatten; (see p. 17). Mince then mix with **1** and **2** ; marinate 10 minutes.

2 Heat 4 T. oil. Stir-fry stems until separated; remove and mix with ham and marinated **2** to make filling. Place one portion of filling in a dumpling skin. Fold in the two ends and seal the edge of the skin with water. Follow the same procedure for the remaining dumplings.

3 Heat 1 T. oil in a non-stick pan; arrange dumplings in the pan. Fry over medium heat for 30 seconds; add mixture **3** . Cook over high heat 8 minutes until water evaporates. Reduce heat to low and cook until bottom of dumpling turns brown. Invert in a plate. Serve with **4** .

1 香菇蒂泡軟搥扁(見17頁)，剁碎，拌入 **1** 料及 **2** 料混合醃10分鐘備用。

2 油4大匙燒熱，入香菇蒂炒開，鏟出與素火腿丁及醃好的 **2** 料拌勻成餡。將餡逐一包入水餃皮內，折合邊緣並用水黏緊。

3 平底鍋(不黏鍋)內放油1大匙，將鍋貼排好，中火煎約30秒，隨入調勻的 **3** 料大火煮至水乾約8分鐘，改小火煮至鍋貼底部微黃。倒扣盤上，沾 **4** 料食用。

2 preserved eggs (Fig. 1)

2 salty egg yolks

2 salty egg whites, beaten
4 eggs, beaten
$\frac{1}{2}$ c. fresh soybeans (Fig. 2)
  or green peas
2 T. milk

1 T. sesame oil

皮蛋(圖1) ·····················	2個
生鹹蛋黃 ·····················	2個
1 生鹹蛋白(打散) ··············	2個
蛋(打散) ·····················	4個
毛豆*或青豆仁 ··············	1/2杯
牛奶 ·························	2大匙
麻油 ·························	1大匙

Rainbow Steamed Eggs

五彩蒸蛋

1 Cut each preserved egg and salty egg yolk into 4 portions. Mix with **1** then put in a container.

2 Bring water to boil. Reduce heat to low and steam egg mixture 20 minutes. Turn off heat and let stand for 2 minutes. Remove the container, invert, and cut the mixture in pieces; sprinkle with sesame oil.

■ To remove eggs easily: spread oil inside the container, lay in a sheet of cellophane, spread on oil again, pour in egg mixture, then steam.

1 將皮蛋、鹹蛋黃每個切4；拌入 **1** 料再倒入容器內。

2 水燒開，用中小火蒸20分鐘後熄火，燜2分鐘取出，倒扣出來切塊，淋上麻油即成。

■ 先在容器內抹油放置玻璃紙，再抹油，才放入蛋液，可使蒸好的蛋較易倒出。

★ 毛豆(圖2)是新鮮的黃豆。

½ lb. (225g) vegetarian meat *, sliced

1 slice carrot, cut in flower shape

4 T. butter

½ lb. (225g) dried mustard cabbage, presoftened & minced

1
1 T. each: sugar, cornstarch
1 t. soy sauce
2 T. vegetarian stock or water

1 t. sesame oil

素五花肉*(切片)　6兩(225公克)

紅蘿蔔(切圓花片)　…………1片

奶油　………………………4大匙

梅乾菜(泡軟、切碎)　………6兩
　　　　　　　　　　　　(225公克)

糖、太白粉　……………各1大匙
醬油　………………………1小匙
素高湯或水　………………2大匙

麻油　………………………1小匙

Meat & Mustard Cabbage

梅菜素肉

1　Spread oil inside of a bowl then place carrots in the center. Heat 1 T. oil; stir-fry meat briefly. Remove; arrange around the carrot.

2　Melt butter in wok; stir-fry cabbage briefly. Add mixture **1** , stir-fry; then pour in bowl. Steam over high heat and boiling water 15 minutes. Invert the bowl on a plate; sprinkle with sesame oil. Serve with bread if desired.

*　Vegetarian meat (Fig. 1) is made by coating gluten rolls with soy sauce.

1　碗內塗油，放上紅蘿蔔花備用。油1大匙燒熱，入素五花肉略炒，盛出排在碗內。

2　奶油放入鍋內待溶化，將梅乾菜略炒，隨入調勻的 **1** 料炒拌，也倒入碗內，水燒開大火蒸15分鐘，倒扣在盤上，淋麻油即可；適於夾饅頭或麵包。

*　素五花肉(圖1)是麵筋用醬油著色製成的。

10 slices toast

5 slices American vegetarian
   ham*

10 slices lotus root (Fig. 2)

2 T. honey
2 t. crushed rock candy or sugar
1 T. cornstarch
2 t. water

54

1

Ham & Lotus Root

蜜藕火腿

土司麵包	10片
美國素火腿 *	5片
蓮藕 **	10片
1 ⎰ 蜂蜜	2大匙
碎冰糖或白糖	2小匙
太白粉	1大匙
水	2小匙

1 Remove crust from each slice of toast then cut in half (makes 20 slices). Cut ham in half to make 10 slices.

2 Heat 1 T. oil; fry both sides of vegetarian ham until hot. Remove; arrange with lotus in a container. Pour on mixture **1** . Steam in boiling water over high heat for 12 minutes. Remove the container and invert it on a plate. Serve the ham mixture with bread.

★ American vegetarian ham (Fig. 1) is suitable for sandwiches and goes well with fried rice.

1 將每片麵包去邊切半，可切成 20 片；每片素火腿切半，可切成 10 片。

2 油 1 大匙燒熱，將素火腿兩面煎熱後鏟出與蓮藕排在容器內，淋上調勻的 **1** 料；水燒開大火蒸約 12 分鐘取出，倒扣在盤上，夾麵包食用。

★ 美國素火腿 (圖 1) 色澤紅，具燻味，適做三明治、炒飯。

★ ★ 蓮藕 (圖 2) 為蓮花的地下莖。

1 1 T. minced cedar leaves*
total of ¼ lb. (115g), diced: presoftened Chinese black mushrooms, American vegetarian
ham*, bamboo shoots or
jicama

2 t. soy sauce

2 2 T. chick peas (Fig. 1)
1 T. presoftened dried black
moss**
1 ½ T. minced Szechwan pickled
mustard greens*
2 eggs, beaten

3 ½ lb. (225g) mashed soft tofu
½ t. salt
⅓ c. water
2 t. cornstarch

2 t. sesame oil

Baked Tofu

香烤豆腐

1	香椿＊(切碎) …………………1大匙 香菇(泡軟)、美國素火腿＊、冬筍 或涼薯……切丁共3兩(115公克)	
	醬油 …………………………2小匙	
2	鷄豆(圖1) ……………………2大匙 髮菜＊＊(泡好的) …………1大匙 榨菜＊(不泡水) ……切碎1 1/2大匙 蛋(打散) ……………………2個	
3	嫩豆腐(壓碎) ……6兩(225公克) 鹽 ………………………………1/2小匙 水 ………………………………1/3杯 太白粉 ………………………2小匙	
	麻油 …………………………2小匙	

1. Heat 1 T. oil. Stir-fry **1** until fragrant; add soy sauce, stir and then remove. Mix well with **2** and **3** . Pour in a greased container, cover with aluminum foil.

2. Preheat the oven to 450˚ F (240˚ C); bake 25 minutes (or steam). Remove and invert on a plate. Sprinkle with sesame oil.

★ See p. 69 for cedar leaves; p. 55 for American vegetarian ham and p. 73 for Szechwan pickled mustard greens.

★★ Dried black moss (Fig. 2) grows in the desert and contains a lot of sand; wash thoroughly before use.

1. 油1大匙燒熱,將 **1** 料炒香,加醬油炒拌盛出,與 **2** 料及 **3** 料拌勻,倒入塗油的容器內,蓋上鋁箔紙。

2. 烤箱燒熱,以450 ℉ (240 ℃)烤或蒸25分鐘取出倒扣在盤上,淋上麻油即可。

★ 香椿見69頁＊,美國素火腿見55頁,榨菜見73頁。

★★ 髮菜(圖2)因生長在沙漠,多沙,需洗乾淨才使用。

$^2/_3$ lb. (300g) minced bean curd pouch (see p. 29) or mashed tofu

1
$^1/_4$ lb. (115g) minced potatoes
1 minced water chestnut
2 beaten eggs
$^1/_4$ t. salt
1 T. minced ginger root

2
1 sheet nori (see p. 73), hand shredded
6 T. each: cornstarch, flour

oil for deep-frying

新鮮腐皮(見29頁,切碎)
或豆腐(壓碎) ……8兩(300公克)
1 馬鈴薯(切碎) ……3兩(115公克)
荸薺(切碎) …………………1個
蛋(打散) …………………2個
鹽 ……………………¼小匙
薑(切碎) …………………1大匙

2 紫菜(見73頁,撕碎) ………1張
太白粉、麵粉 …………各6大匙

炸油 …………………………適量

Bean Curd Balls

素炸魚球

1　Stir **1** briefly to mix. Add mixture **2** ; stir to mix well. Divide and roll into 12 balls.

2　Heat oil for deep-frying. Fry the balls over medium heat 6 minutes until golden brown; remove. Serve with dipping sauce.

■　To make dipping sauce: Mix well, 1 T. ketchup, 1 t. each of water and miso, and 2 t. ginger root juice.

1　將 **1** 料略拌,再加混合的 **2** 料拌勻揉成12個丸子。

2　炸油燒熱,用中火將丸子炸呈金黃色約6分鐘撈出,與沾料食用。

■　沾料做法:將番茄醬1大匙,味噌、水各1小匙,薑汁2小匙拌勻即成。

½ lb. (225g) gluten rolls*

2 T. sweet bean paste
2 T. tomato sauce
1 c. beet juice (beet, see p. 15)
½ t. five spice powder
¼ t. pepper
3 slices ginger root

oil for deep-frying

1 T. white sesame

麵筋 * ···············6兩（225公克）

甜麵醬 ······················2大匙
番茄調味汁 ·················2大匙
紅甜菜汁（見15頁，擠出汁） 1杯
五香粉 ·····················¹/₂小匙
胡椒 ·······················¹/₄小匙
薑 ·························3片

炸油 ·························適量

白芝麻 ·····················1大匙

Vegetarian Barbecued Pork

素味叉燒

1 Bring gluten rolls and ¹ to boil. Cook 5 minutes; remove gluten rolls. Stir-fry sesame until fragrant; remove.

2 Heat oil for deep-frying. Fry cooked gluten rolls over high heat for 2 minutes. Remove; diagonally slice them. Sprinkle with white sesame seeds. Serve.

★ Gluten rolls (Fig. 1) are made of flour.

1 將麵筋放入 ¹ 料內燒開，煮5分鐘，麵筋入味即撈出。芝麻炒香備用。

2 炸油燒熱，用大火將煮好的麵筋炸2分鐘取出，切斜片撒上白芝麻即成。

★ 麵筋（圖1）的原料爲麵粉，是一種高筋性的植物蛋白質。

1. 1 T. cedar leaves (see p. 69, minced) or minced ginger root
5 Chinese black mushrooms (presoftened, shredded)

1 T. soy sauce

2. total of ⅔ lb. (300g), cut in pieces: nappa cabbage or cabbage, carrot
10 fried gluten puffs (Fig. 1)
6 Chinese black mushroom balls
6 vegetarian fish cakes, sliced

6 c. vegetarian stock (see p. 5)

3. 2 oz. (50g) bean threads (presoftened, cut in half)
1 t. salt

2 eggs

1

香椿(見69頁，切碎)或
薑末 ……………………1大匙
香菇(泡軟，切絲) …………5朵

醬油 ……………………1大匙

山東白菜或高麗菜，紅蘿蔔
(切塊) ……………8兩(300公克)
油麵筋泡(圖1) ……………10粒
香菇脆丸 ……………………6粒
素甜不辣(切片) ……………6條

素高湯(見5頁)……………6杯

粉絲1小把 ………1.5兩(50公克)
(泡軟，略切)
鹽 ……………………………1小匙

蛋 ……………………………2個

Vegetarian Mix

大鍋菜

1   Heat 3 T. oil. Stir-fry **1** until fragrant then add soy sauce; stir-fry briefly. Add **2** and stir-fry 1 minute. Add stock and bring to boil. Reduce heat to medium; continue to cook 5 minutes. Add **3** ; bring to another boil. Add eggs and boil until cooked.

1   油3大匙燒熱，炒香 **1** 料，入醬油略炒，續入 **2** 料炒1分鐘，加高湯燒開，改中火煮5分鐘，放入 **3** 料再燒開，加蛋煮至蛋熟即成。

1
3 presoftened Chinese black
   mushrooms
¼ c. vegetarian meat shreds (see
   p. 75)
2 T. shredded ginger root

2
1 package dried black moss (see
   p. 57)
1 c. shredded tofu
½ c. shredded bamboo shoots

5 c. vegetarian stock (see p. 5)

3
3 T. each: cornstarch, water

4
¾ t. salt
¼ t. pepper
2 t. sesame oil
2 T. each: soy sauce, minced
   coriander

1	香菇 ……3朵，素肉絲……¹/₄杯 薑(切絲) ………………2大匙
2	髮菜 …………………1小包 豆腐(切絲) ………………1杯 筍絲 ……………………¹/₂杯
	素高湯(見5頁) …………5杯
3	太白粉，水 …………各3大匙
4	鹽……³/₄小匙，胡椒 ……¹/₄小匙 麻油 ……………………2小匙 醬油、香菜末 ………各2大匙

Meat & Black Moss Soup
髮菜香羹

1 Separately soak Chinese black mushrooms, vegetarian meat shreds, black moss in water until soft. Shred the mushrooms.

2 Heat 2 T. oil. Stir-fry **1** until fragrant; add **2** and vegetarian stock. Bring to boil; add mixture **3** to thicken then **4** . Serve.

1 香菇、素肉絲(見75頁)、髮菜(見57頁)均泡軟，香菇切絲備用。

2 油2大匙燒熱，炒香 **1** 料，隨入 **2** 料及高湯燒開，再加調勻的 **3** 料勾成薄汁，最後加入 **4** 料即成。

Shark Fin Soup
素魚翅羹

1 Use total 2/3 lb. (300g) of shredded cabbage, mushrooms, presoftened wood ears and carrots for **1** . Use 1/2 c. vegetarian shark fins (Fig. 1) (presoftened) for **2** . Add vinegar to **4** . Other procedures are the same as above recipe.

1 將 **1** 料改用高麗菜、洋菇、泡軟的木耳、紅蘿蔔，切絲共8兩(300公克)； **2** 料改用素魚翅(圖1)¹/₂杯泡軟， **4** 料內加醋，其他做法同上。

2 T. butter

$\frac{1}{2}$ c. sliced vegetarian sausage*

1 total of $\frac{2}{3}$ lb. (300g): mushrooms, cabbage, potatoes, carrots, and tomatoes

$\frac{1}{4}$ c. flour

2 $\frac{3}{4}$ t. salt
$\frac{1}{4}$ t. pepper
5 c. vegetarian stock

$\frac{1}{3}$ c. cooked macaroni

1

奶油 ·················2大匙

素香腸*(切片) ···········1/2杯

1 洋菇、高麗菜、馬鈴薯、紅蘿蔔
番茄········切片共8兩(300公克)

麵粉 ····················1/4杯

2 鹽 ·····················3/4小匙
胡椒 ····················1/4小匙
素高湯 ···················5杯

煮熟的通心粉 ···············1/3杯

Western Cream Soup
西式濃湯

1 Heat 2 T. butter. Stir-fry sausage briefly; add **1** and stir-fry until heated. Add flour; stir. Add **2** ; bring to boil. Reduce heat to medium and continue to cook 5 minutes until vegetables soften, then add macaroni.

★ Vegetarian sausage (Fig. 1) is made of soybeans, flour and Chinese black mushroom stems.

1 奶油2大匙燒熱,入香腸略炒,隨入 **1** 料炒熱,再加麵粉炒拌,續入 **2** 料燒開,改中火煮約5分鐘至蔬菜軟,再入通心粉即成。

★ 素香腸(圖1)是以黃豆、麵粉和菇類爲原料製成的。

3 c. rice

2 eggs, beaten

2 T. cedar leaves*

1 total of 1 ½ c.: vegetarian ham (see p. 33) or vegetarian sausage (see p. 67), chick peas (see p. 57) or canned corn, shredded asparagus (or celery)

2 ½ t. salt
½ T. soy sauce
1 ½ t. sesame oil

68

白飯	⋯⋯⋯⋯⋯⋯3杯
蛋(打散)	⋯⋯⋯⋯⋯⋯2個
香椿*(切碎)	⋯⋯⋯⋯⋯2大匙

1
素火腿(見33頁)
或素香腸(見67頁),
蘆筍或西芹(切丁),
鷄豆(見57頁)或熟玉米粒
⋯⋯⋯⋯⋯⋯⋯⋯共1 1/2杯

2
鹽 ⋯⋯⋯⋯⋯⋯⋯1/2小匙
醬油 ⋯⋯⋯⋯⋯⋯1/2大匙
麻油 ⋯⋯⋯⋯⋯1 1/2小匙

2

Colorful Fried Rice

什錦炒飯

1 Heat 3 T. oil. While scrambling eggs, separate pieces; cook until golden brown. Add cedar leaves and **1** ; stir-fry briefly. Add rice and **2** ; stir 3 minutes until heated and mixed well.

★ Cedar leaves (Fig. 1), basil (Fig. 2), and coriander are interchangeable.

1 油3大匙燒熱,將蛋炒拌使其散開,炒至金黃色,依序入香椿及 **1** 料略炒,再加飯及 **2** 料炒拌至飯熱,材料均勻 (約3分鐘) 即可。

★ 香椿(圖1) 九層塔(圖2) 或香菜,三者均可相互取代。

¹⁄₃ lb. (150g) dried noodles

1 t. brown or black sugar

4 slices ginger root

1 12 vegetarian meat chunks*, pre-
    softened
    6 slices gluten puffs (see p. 43),
    fried

2 1 c. tomato, cut in pieces
    3 T. soy sauce
    3 c. stock or water

green vegetables as desired

3 1 T. cedar leaves or coriander,
    minced
    ¹⁄₂ t. chili pepper or chili paste
    1 t. sesame oil

	乾麵 ················4兩(150公克)	
	紅糖或黑糖 ···············1小匙	
	薑 ····················4片	
1	素肉塊*(泡軟) ············12粒	
	烤麩(見43頁,炸好的) ······6片	
2	番茄(切塊) ················1杯	
	醬油 ···················3大匙	
	素高湯或水 ················3杯	
	靑菜 ····················適量	
3	香椿或香菜(切碎) ·········1大匙	
	辣椒或辣椒醬 ············$^1/_2$小匙	
	麻油 ···················1小匙	

Tomato & Noodles in Broth

茄汁湯麵

1 Heat 2 T. oil. Stir-fry brown sugar in low heat until melted and black. Add ginger root slices; stir-fry for 30 seconds. Add **1** ; stir-fry for 1 minute. Add **2** ; bring to boil over high heat. Continue to cook in medium heat for 10 minutes to complete vegetarian meat soup.

2 Follow instructions on package to cook 1/3 lb. (150g) dried noodles, yielding 1 lb. (450g) cooked noodles. Put the noodles in a bowl; blanch the green vegetables; then place on noodles. Pour in meat soup; sprinkle with **3** . Serve.

★ Vegetarian meat chunks (Fig. 1) are made from soybeans. Soak in water until soft and squeeze out water before use.

1 油2大匙燒熱,用小火將紅糖炒至糖溶化略呈黑色,隨入薑片炒30秒,續入 **1** 料炒1分鐘,再加 **2** 料大火燒開,改中火續煮10分鐘即成素肉湯。

2 乾麵4兩(150公克)依包裝上指示放入滾水內煮熟約12兩(450公克),靑菜燙熟, 放入麵碗內,澆上素肉湯,撒上 **3** 料即成。

★ 素肉塊(圖1)是以大豆爲原料製成的,使用前需泡軟沖洗,擠乾水份使用。

¹/₃ lb. (150g) dried noodles

2 c. green bean sprouts or shredded cabbage

1
2 T. minced Szechwan pickled
mustard greens* or pickled
cabbage
1 T. each: vegetarian sa tsa
sauce (see p. 31), soy sauce
1 T. cooking oil
1 t. sesame oil

2
2 T. minced coriander
1 sheet nori (Fig. 2)

1

乾麵 ·················4兩 (150公克)

綠豆芽或高麗菜絲 ··········2杯

1
榨菜*或雪菜(切碎) ········2大匙
素沙茶醬(見31頁)、醬油各1大匙
沙拉油 ···················1大匙
麻油 ···················1小匙

2
香菜(切碎) ·········2大匙
紫菜(圖2) ···············1張

Nori in Noodles

紫香乾麵

1. Follow instructions on package to cook noodles. Yield will be 1 lb. (450g) of cooked noodles. Blanch bean sprouts. Tear nori to mince size pieces.

2. Mix cooked noodles with bean sprouts and **1** (add water if too dry). Sprinkle with **2** and stir lightly.

★ See Fig. 1, these are made of marinated gai choy stems. Briefly rinse before use.

1. 乾麵依包裝上指示放入滾水內煮熟約12兩(450公克)。綠豆芽燙熟。紫菜撕碎備用。

2. 將煮熟的麵拌入綠豆芽及調勻的 **1** 料(拌時如太乾,可隨意加少許水),再撒上 **2** 料輕拌即成。

★ 榨菜(圖1)是醃漬過的芥菜莖,味鹹香,使用前略洗即可。

1/3 lb. (150g) rice noodles

4 presoftened Chinese black
  mushrooms, shredded

1 T. soy sauce

1 | total of 1/3 lb. (150g), shredded:
  carrots, celery

2 | 1/2 t. salt
pepper as desired
1 t. each: vinegar, sesame oil
1/2 c. vegetarian stock or water

3 | 2 eggs, fried & shredded
1/3 lb. (150g) green bean sprouts

細米粉	....	4兩(150公克)
香菇(泡軟、切絲)	....	4朵
醬油	....	1大匙
1 紅蘿蔔、芹菜	....	切絲共4兩 (150公克)
2 鹽	....	½小匙
胡椒	....	隨意
醋、麻油	....	各1小匙
素高湯或水	....	½杯
3 蛋(煎蛋皮切絲)	....	2個
綠豆芽	....	4兩(150公克)

Rainbow Fried Rice Noodles

五彩米粉

1 Separate rice noodles then soak in cold water 30 minutes; drain.

2 Heat 4 T. oil. Stir-fry mushrooms and soy sauce until fragrant. Add **1**, **2**, and the rice noodles; cover and cook until steamy. Add **3** and stir-fry to mix well.

1 將米粉打散用冷水泡軟約30分鐘，撈出。

2 油4大匙燒熱，依序入香菇及醬油炒香，再入 **1**、**2** 料及泡好的米粉，蓋鍋見水蒸氣冒出加 **3** 料翻炒均勻即成。

Fried Noodles

炒麵

1 Replace rice noodles with dried noodles. Cook 1/3 lb. (150g) noodles, which will expand 3 times after cooking.

2 Other ingredients and procedures are the same as above recipe except no need to cover because noodles are already cooked. Presoftened vegetarian meat (Fig. 1) and Chinese black mushrooms may be used for eggs.

1 乾麵條4兩(150公克)煮熟後，重約增3倍。

2 做法同上，唯因麵條是熟的，加料後不必加蓋炒拌均勻即可。如不用蛋，可加素肉絲(圖1)泡軟與香菇同炒。

4 buns

1 c. Chinese black mushroom
   stems

1
total of ¼ lb. (115g), minced:
   potato, gluten rolls (see p. 61)
2 eggs, beaten
2 T. cornstarch
½ t. salt
½ t. basil powder or five spice
   powder
2 t. soy sauce
1 t. sesame oil

2
4 slices of each: tomato, cheese,
   lettuce
8 slices pickle
4 T. mayonnaise

圓型麵包 ……………………4個

乾香菇蒂 ……………………1杯

馬鈴薯、麵筋(見61頁)
………………切碎共3兩(115公克)
蛋(打散) ……………………2個
太白粉 ……………………2大匙
1 鹽 ……………………¹/₂小匙
九層粉或五香粉 …………¹/₂小匙
醬油 ……………………2小匙
麻油 ……………………1小匙

番茄、起士、生菜 ………各4片
2 酸黃瓜 ……………………8片
美乃滋 ……………………4大匙

Hamburger

素味漢堡

1 Soften mushroom stems in water then flatten (see p. 17). Mince and mix with **1** evenly; divide and make 4 patties.

2 Heat 4 T. oil. Fry patties over medium heat 2 minutes on each side. Turn them over again and fry for another 2 minutes on each side until golden brown (total about 8 minutes).

3 Place patties and **2** in buns. Serve.

1 香菇蒂泡軟搥扁(見17頁),再剁碎與 **1** 料拌勻,做成四個圓餅。

2 油4大匙燒熱,用中火將圓餅兩面各煎2分鐘,再翻過來兩面各煎2分鐘(計約8分鐘)呈金黃色。

3 將煎好的餅放在麵包內,鋪上1份 **2** 料即可食用。

□ Index

索引

More From Wei-Chuan Publishing 味全叢書

Cookbooks :
(All cookbooks are bilingual English/Chinese unless footnoted otherwise)

Chinese Appetizers & Garnishes
Chinese Cooking, Favorite Home Dishes
Chinese Cooking For Beginners (Revised) [1]
Chinese Cooking Made Easy
Chinese Cuisine
Chinese Cuisine-Szechwan Style
Chinese Cuisine-Taiwanese Style
Chinese Dim Sum
Chinese One Dish Meals
Chinese Seafood [2]
Chinese Snacks (Revised)
Favorite Chinese Dishes
Great Garnishes
Healthful Cooking
Japanese Cuisine
Low Cholesterol Chinese Cuisine
Mexican Cooking Made Easy [3]
Microwave Cooking I, Chinese Style
Microwave Cooking II, Chinese Style
Noodles, Chinese Home-Cooking
Noodles, Classical Chinese Cooking
Rice, Chinese Home-Cooking
Rice, Traditional Chinese Cooking
Thai Cooking Made Easy
Vegetarian Cooking

Small Cookbook Series :
Vegetables [2]
Beef [2]
Chicken [2]
Tofu! Tofu! Tofu!
Very! Very! Vegetarian!
Soup! Soup! Soup!

Carving Tools

Videos [4] :
Chinese Garnishes I
Chinese Garnishes II
Chinese Stir-Frying, Beef
Chinese Stir-Frying, Chicken
Chinese Stir-Frying, Vegetables

1 Also available in English/Spanish,
   French/Chinese, and German/Chinese
2 English and Chinese are
   separate editions
3 Also available in English/Spanish
4 English only

食譜系列
（如無數字標註，即為中英對照版）

拼盤與盤飾
實用家庭菜
實用中國菜 [1] （修訂版）
速簡中國菜
中國菜
四川菜
台灣菜
飲茶食譜
簡餐專輯
海鮮專輯 [2]
點心專輯
家常100
盤飾精選
健康食譜
日本料理
均衡飲食
墨西哥菜 [3]
微波爐食譜
微波爐食譜II
麵，家常篇
麵，精華篇
米食，家常篇
米食，傳統篇
泰國菜
素食

味全小食譜：
牛肉 [2]
雞肉 [2]
蔬菜 [2]
豆腐
家常素食
湯

雕花刀

錄影帶 [4]
盤飾I
盤飾II
炒菜入門，牛肉
炒菜入門，雞肉
炒菜入門，蔬菜

1 中英、中法、中德、英西
2 中文版及英文版
3 中英版及英西版
4 英文版

Wei-Chuan Cookbooks can be purchased in the U.S.A., Canada and twenty other countries worldwide • Wei-Chuan Publishing • 1455 Monterey Pass Road, #1
Monterey Park, CA 91754, U.S.A. • Tel: (213)261-3880 • Fax: (213) 261-3299
味全食譜在台、美、加及全球二十餘國皆有發行 • 味全出版社有限公司 • 台北市仁愛路4段28號2樓 • Tel: (02) 702-1148 • Fax: (02) 704-2729